HOME NUMBER ONE

RMC   Baraitser, Marion
940.42   Home number one
BAR

18386

Thanks to my lovely husband Michael who helped to bring this book to fruition, and to all my grandchildren who taught me to read comics intelligently.

Thanks also to Simon Bayly, Corinne Pearlman, and Lily Herzberg for their input, ideas and inspiration.

Fifteen thousand children passed through the Nazi transit camp Thereseinstadt. One hundred survived.

This book is dedicated to them.

HOME NUMBER ONE

A graphic novel

MARION BARAITSER   ANNA EVANS

A modern teenager's life-changing journey

LOKI BOOKS
www.lokibooks.com

LOKI BOOKS

www.lokibooks.com

First published in Great Britain as a Loki Books paperback original in 2006 by
LOKI BOOKS LTD, 38 Chalcot Crescent, London NW1 8YD

Copyright © text by Marion Baraitser, 38 Chalcot Crescent, London NW1 8YD

Copyright © cover and drawings by Anna Evans, 193a Symonds Street, Newton, Auckland, New Zealand.

All rights reserved. No part of the publication may be reproduced, stored in a retrieval system, or transmitted, in any form or by any other means, electronic, mechanical, photocopying, recording or otherwise, without the prior permission of the copyright owner.

Printed and bound by Antony Rowe Ltd, Bumper's Farm, Chippenham, Wiltshire SN14 6LH

A CIP catalogue record for this book is available from the British Library.

Cover design by Anna Evans

ISBN LOKI 0 952942674

Speak You Also
by
Paul Celan
(tr Michael Hamburger)

Speak, you also,
speak as the last,
have your say.

Speak —
But keep yes and no unsplit.
And give your say this meaning:
give it the shade.

Give it shade enough,
give it as much
as you know has been dealt out between
midnight and midday and midnight.

Look around:
look how it all leaps alive —
where death is! Alive!
He speaks truly who speaks the shade.

But now shrinks the place where you stand:
Where now, stripped by shade, will you go?
Upward. Grope your way up.
Thinner you grow, less knowable, finer.
Finer: a thread by which
it wants to be lowered, the star:
to float farther down, down below
where it sees itself gleam: in the swell
of wandering words.

from *Selected Poems* (Penguin Twentieth-century Classics)

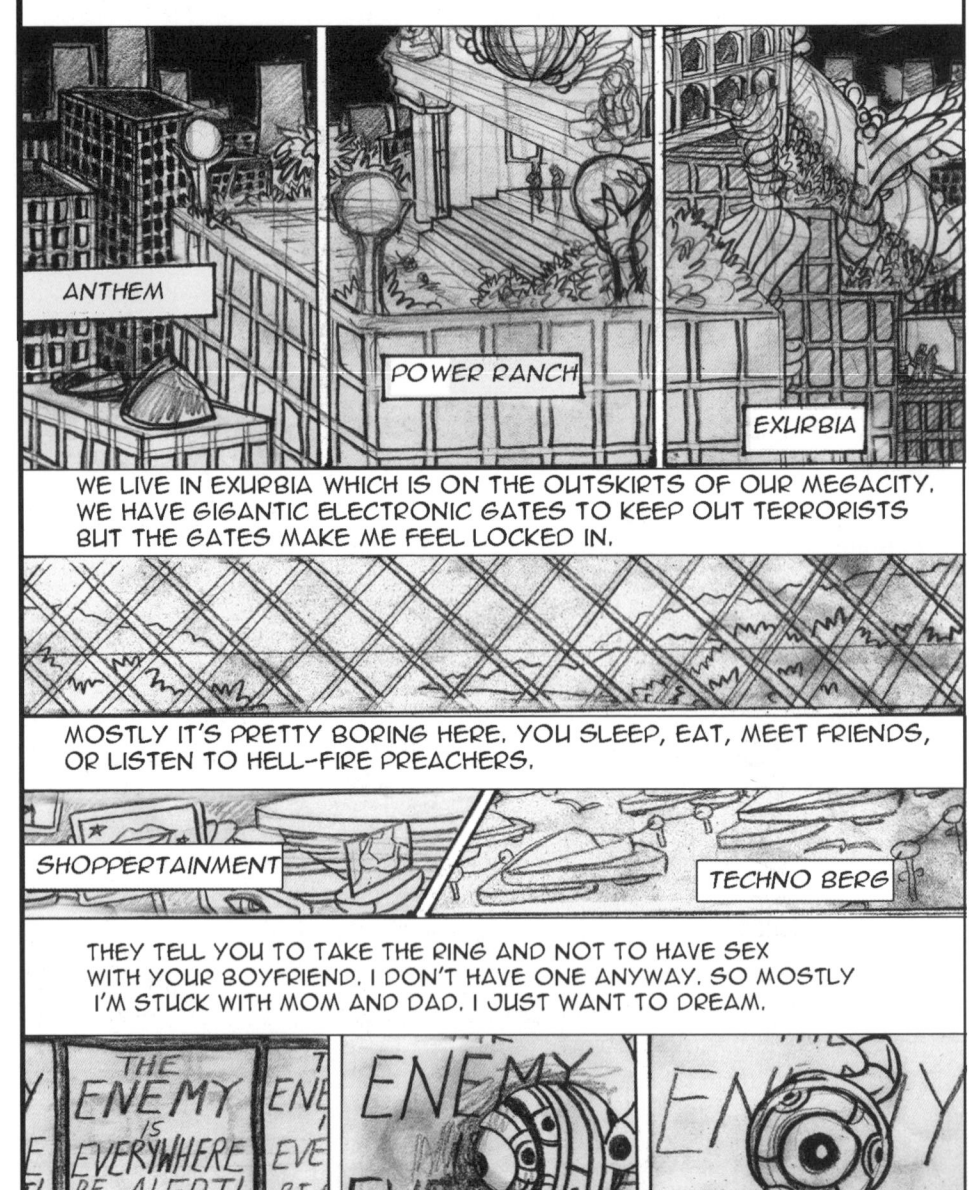

'THIS IS THERESIENSTADT. THEY TELL US IT'S OUR JEWISH PARADISE. IT FEELS LIKE THE END OF THE WORLD WITH THOUSANDS OF US CROWDED INTO A HUGE CAMP. NO ONE EXPLAINS ANYTHING. THEY JUST SET THEIR DOGS ON US.'

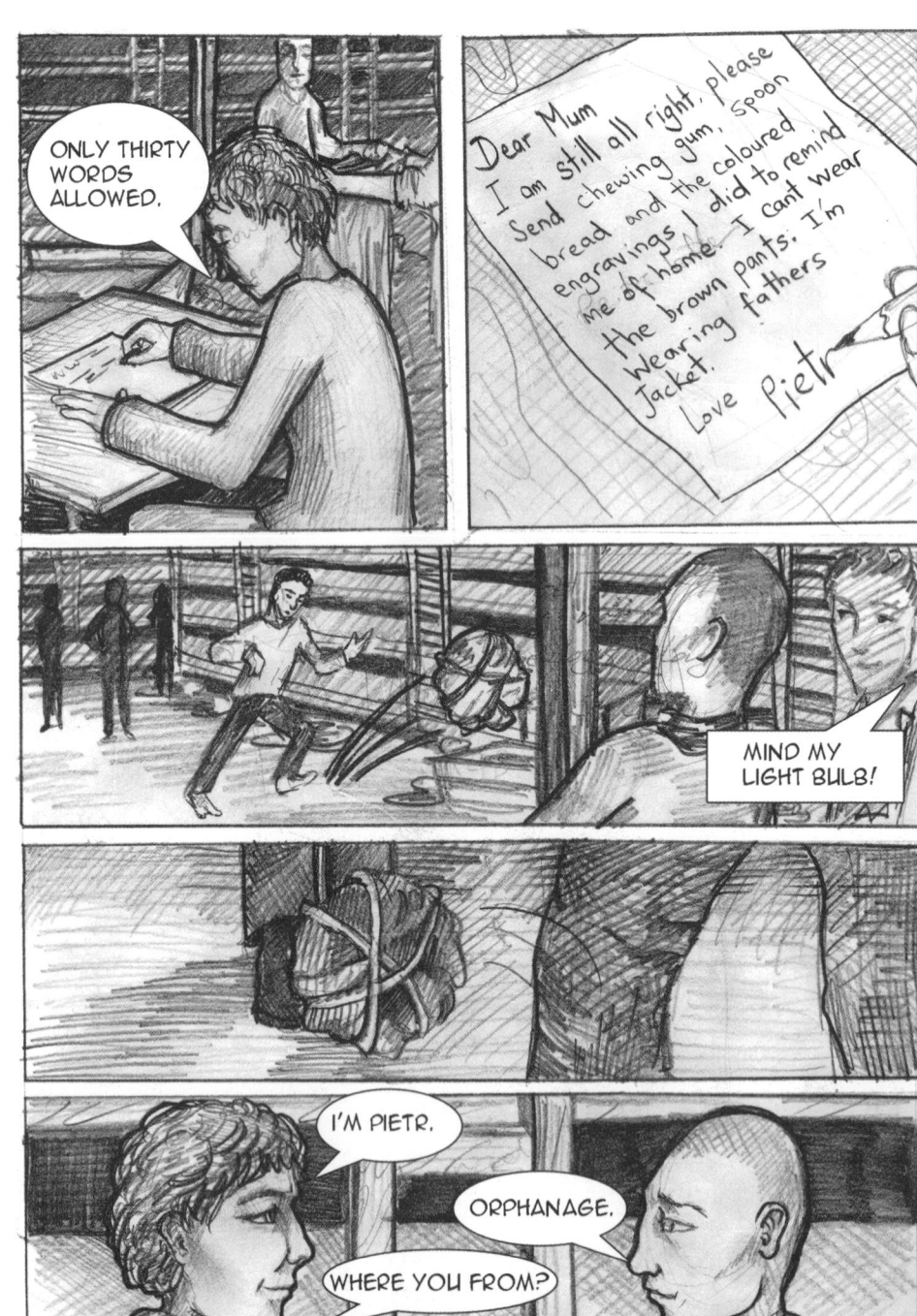

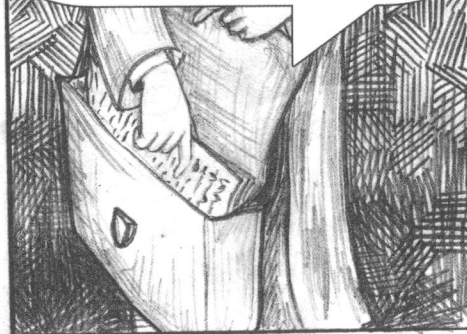

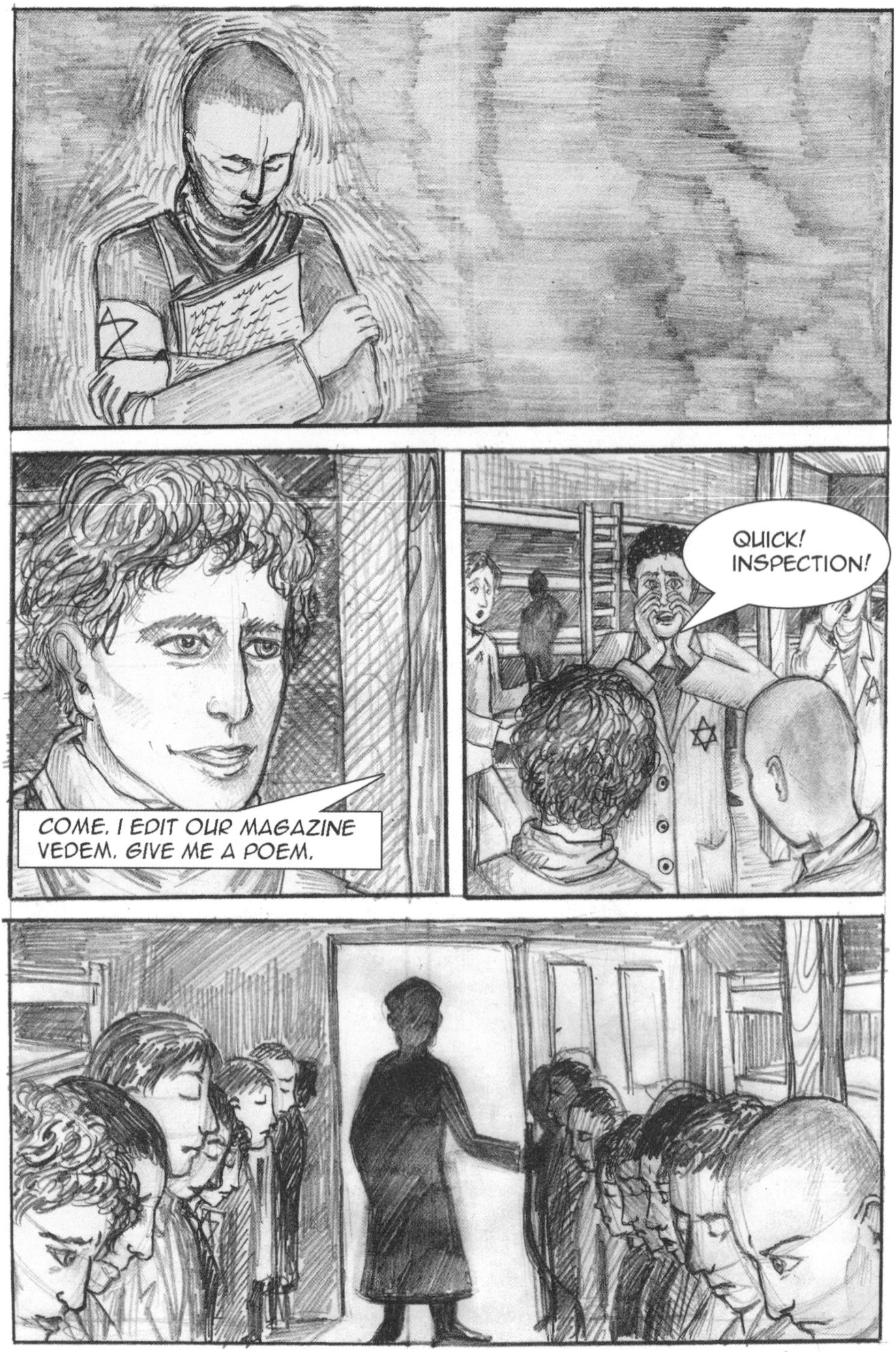

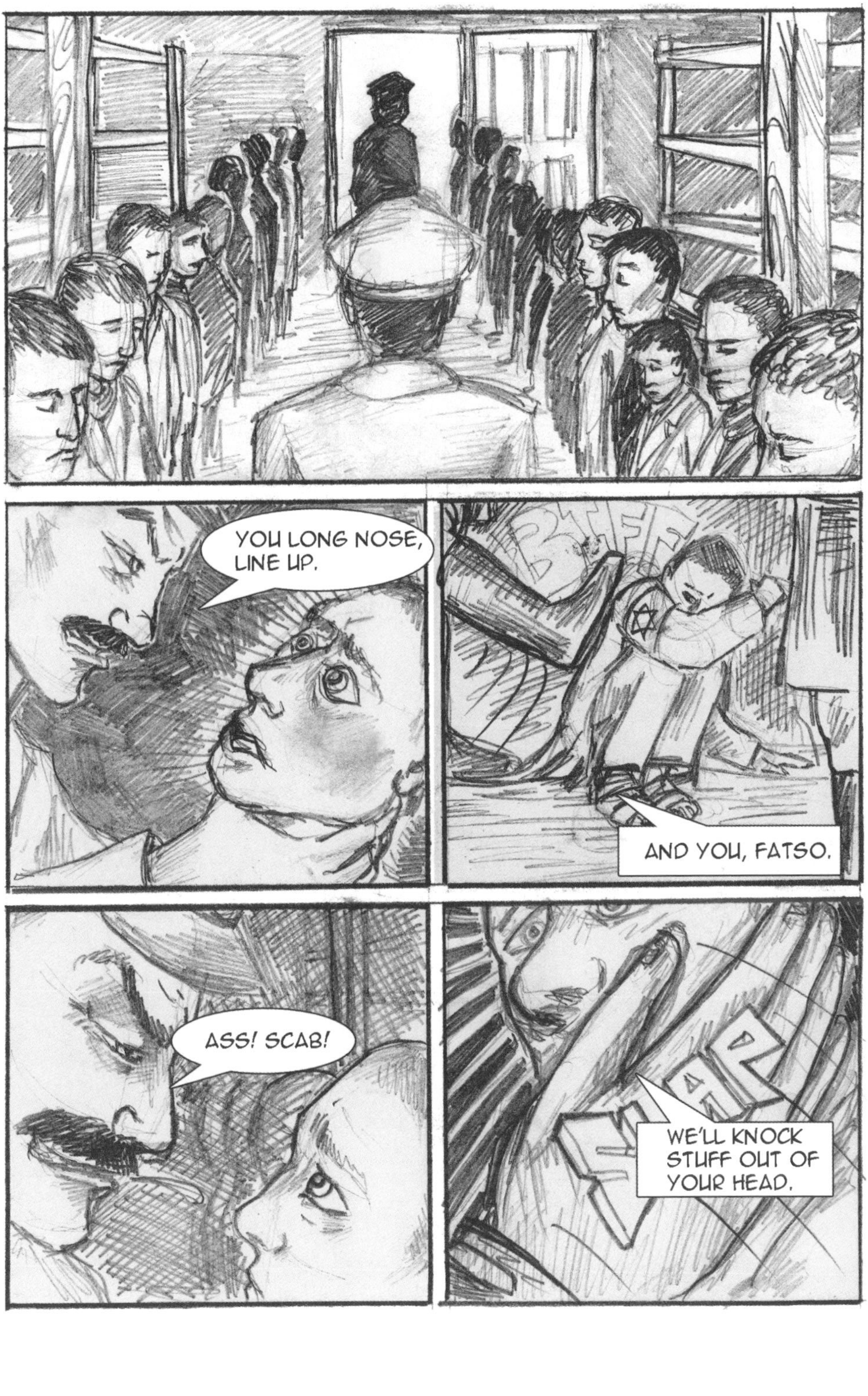

SEE THE LIGHT CAUGHT IN THE TREE? IT'S GOD.

NO, IT'S THE MOON. THE WORLD TURNS BUT WE LIVE LIKE RATS. ONLY THE CLOUDS MOVE ON.

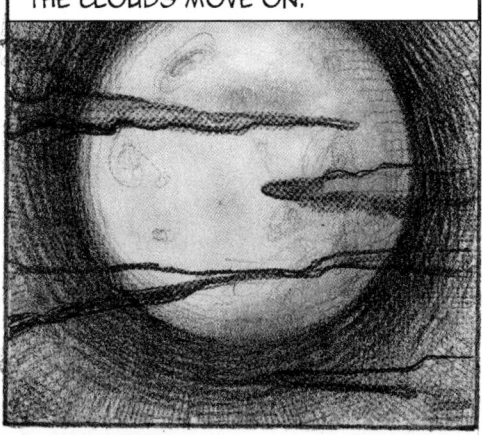

'I WANT TO LIVE, SEE MY HOME AGAIN. LOOK! I'M FLYING THERE. I'M LEAVING MY BODY. I'M BIG, MILES HIGH. ALL MY HEAVINESS IS OUTSIDE ME. NOW I TOUCH HEAVEN. IT'S SHINING, BUT I'M ALONE IN EVERYTHING.'

SO LEARNING IS FORBIDDEN HERE?

TIME FOR MATHS LESSON.

WHO'S ON LOOKOUT?

'MATHS IS PARADISE. YOU LIFT AWAY FROM THE SQUABBLES, THE HUNGER PAINS. TO LEARN IS A MIRACLE! PEOPLE COME TO TEACH US. JIRI SCHORCH ACTED A WHOLE PLAY FOR US FROM MEMORY. BENO KAUFMANN TALKED ABOUT HINDUISM, AND GIDEON KLEIN SPOKE ABOUT HIS MUSIC. ALL ARE GONE!'

WE'LL DO SOME DRAWING. USE PAPER SACKS. CHARCOAL FROM THE STOVES.
LICHTSPERRE! LIGHTS OUT.
NO BUTTERFLIES IN HERE.
DRAW A BLANK WALL.
DRAW A BUTTERFLY BEHIND BARS.
THE CHOIR ARE DOING BRUNDIBAR AGAIN IN THE ATTIC. WE ALL KNOW WHO THAT NASTY ORGAN GRINDER IS! LOOK HOW HE STEALS FROM CHILDREN! SING WITH THE CHOIR.
'BRUNDIBAR BEATEN IS RUNNING AWAY. STRIKE THE DRUM, WE'VE WON THE WAR. WE'VE WON ONLY BECAUSE WE DIDN'T GIVE UP, BECAUSE WE WEREN'T AFRAID, BECAUSE WE ALL SANG OUR MARCHING SONG!'

HOME NUMBER ONE.
WHO CAN SLEEP?
IN THIS SWAMP.
MAYBE WE'LL SEE A WHITE HORSE FOR LUCK.
WE COULD GO TO THE TREE. HAVE A GOOD SWING.
BUUUUURRP
COUGH
FART
HEY! WHAT'S THE MATTER WITH HIM?
HE'S PALE. COME AND TAKE A LOOK.

HE'S ASLEEP.
SLIPPING AWAY.
SHALL I WAKE HIM? I HAVE A PIECE OF BREAD.
HE CAN'T HEAR US.
BLOOD!
I MUST GIVE HIM MY BLOOD.
STILL AS A STATUE.
IVAN. COME QUICKLY.
NEVER TOUCHED A DEAD BODY BEFORE.
HELP ME TO THE CREMATORIUM. IT'S SAFE. SS GUARDS DON'T WALK HERE. TYPHOID.

LITTLE PUFF OF SMOKE.
YOU ARE, THEN YOU AREN'T ANYMORE.
CAREFUL.
THE SEDER IS ABOUT DELIVERANCE FROM SLAVERY.
DO YOU BELIEVE?

MY BACK IS HURTING.
WE MUST KEEP GOING.
IT FEELS LIKE I'VE ALWAYS KNOWN YOU.
LOOK. A LUCKY FOUR-LEAVED CLOVER.
WE'RE GOING TO SURVIVE.
WHAT DO YOU WISH FOR MOST?
I WISH I C OULD WALK FREE IN THE CLEAN WORLD. OR STAND IN THE SUN WITH GRANDMA.
I'M SO HUNGRY. QUICK. HIDE THESE.
BUT WE COULD BE SENT EAST!

CZECH POLICE!
DUMP ANY BOOTY. SS FEMALE 'VULTURES' WILL NAB YOU.
THANKS FOR TELLING US.
THERE ARE THOSE TWO GORGEOUS BOYS.
LOOK HOW THEY MAKE THEM PULL THAT HEAVY CART.
THE KOMMANDANT! THERE ARE RUMOUR HE PLANS TO BEAUTIFY THE CAMP FOR A RED CROSS VISIT. HE'S BEGINNING TO BE SCARED OF LOSING.
THAT'S ARIE. I'M GOING TO SAY HELLO. I MUST!

THIS IS PARADISE! I'M AS RED AS A A BEETROOT.
DO WE KNOW EACH OTHER?
I'M DINAH.
WHERE CAN WE MEET PROPERLY?
HERE. BEFORE CURFEW.
IT'S QUIETER THAN MOST PLACES.
I NEED SOMETHING TO WEAR.
NOT THIS STAINED SKIRT.
BOOT
BOOT POLISH!
BE CAREFUL.
BABIES... THEY TAKE THEM AWAY.
DON'T STAY LONGER THAN THE CURFEW. YOU DON'THAVE A PASS, REMEMBER.

WHY AM I SO SHY?
WHY CAN'T I BE MORE SOPHISTICATED?
HEY! WHAT ARE YOU DOING?
BE CAREFUL. THAT'S THE KOMMANDANT'S GARDEN.
WHAT HAVE YOU DONE?
ONE DAY I'LL GIVE YOU EVERYTHING YOU NEED. THEN YOU WON'T BE SO THIN.
STAY WITH ME. I MAY NOT BE HERE TOMORROW. THERE IS NO ONE TO REMEMBER ME.
I HARDLY KNOW YOU. I'M AFRAID.

OUR VOICES JUST ECHO IN THE HUGE VOID. CAN'T YOU HEAR? THE RUSTLING... IT NEVER STOPS.
YOU'RE SHIVVERING. LET ME WARM YOU.
I MUST FORGET MYSELF ESCAPE INTO A KIND OF NIGHT.
YOU THINK TOO MUCH. I DON'T WANT TO ESCAPE. I WANT TO BE HERE, FULLY CONSCIOUS.
WHAT HAVE I MADE OF MY LIFE? THERE'S ONLY WAITING AND FORGETTING.
THERE'S YOUR WRITING.
DO YOU HEAR THE PLANES? THE ALLIES... MAYBE LIFE IS WAITING FOR US.
EVEN IF SOMETHING HAPPENED TO ME, I BELONG HERE WITH YOU.
WE HAVE SO LITTLE TIME.
LOVE ME!
I CAN'T. I MUST BE RESPONSIBLE. IF YOU BECOME PREGNANT...

I HAVE SUCH A YEARNING...
MAYBE DEATH IS THE FINAL FREEDOM. ITS INFINITY. I CAN GIVE MYSELF UP TO IT.
NO! THIS TINY MOMENT OF TOGETHERNESS IS ENOUGH.
WE MUST LIVE. THAT'S OUR POWER.
TAKE RESPONSIBILITY FOR ONE ANOTHER.
COME. GONDA AND PIETR ARE WAITING FOR US IN THE SQUARE.
THE GHETTO SWINGERS ARE PLAYING THERE.
HOW I LONG TO PLAY THE PIANO AGAIN.

'THE WORST IS WHEN THEY DELIVER ONE OF THOSE NASTY STRIPS OF PAPER ORDERING ONE OF US TO THE STATION TO GO EAST.'
BAM!
THEY PLACE THE PAPER ON YOUR BED...
I DON'T WANT TO GO.
'TRANSPORT'! WHAT DOES IT MEAN?
I HEARD IT'S GOING TO AUSCHWITZ.
THEY VANISH INTO THE NIGHT.

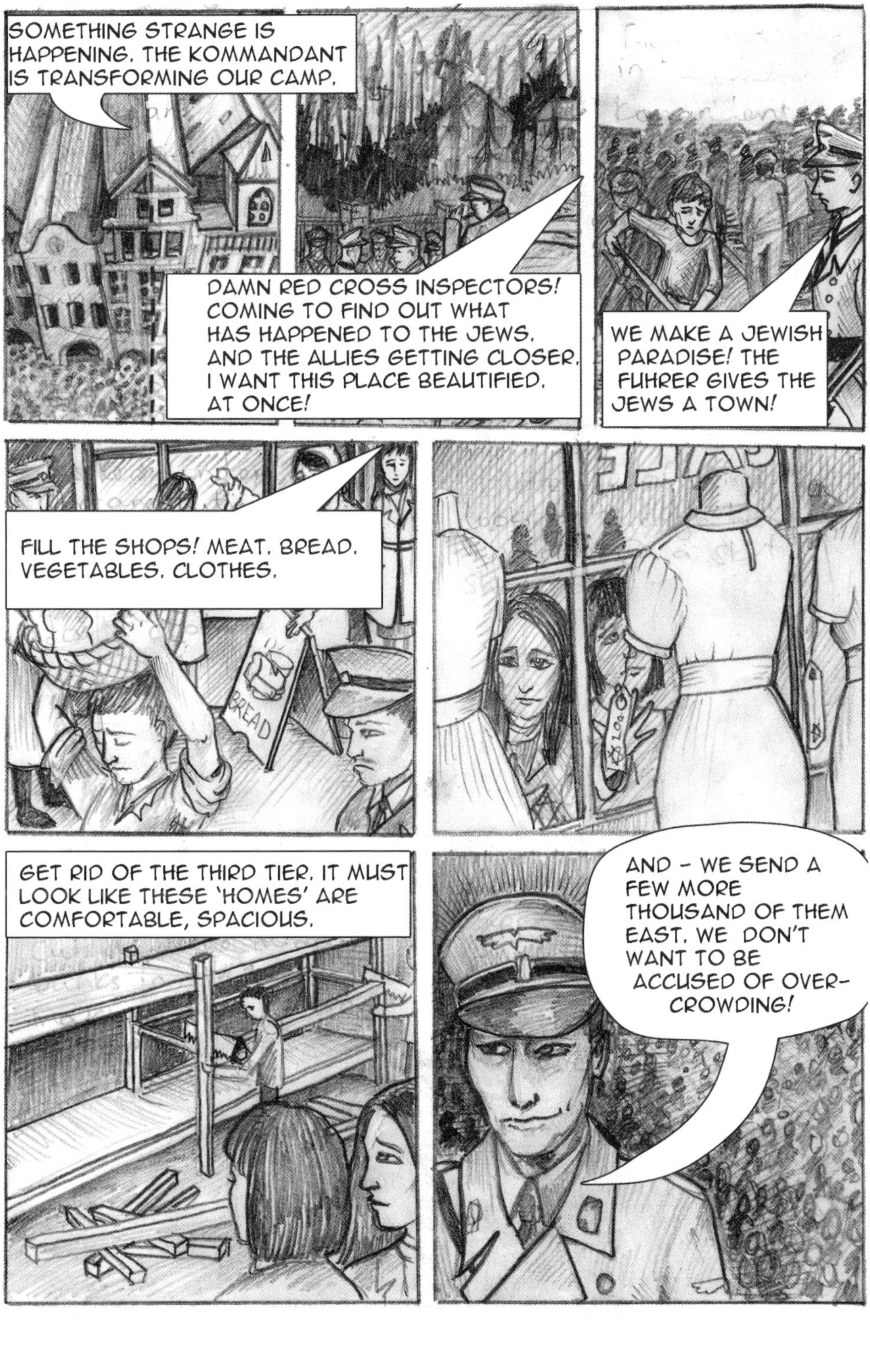
SOMETHING STRANGE IS HAPPENING. THE KOMMANDANT IS TRANSFORMING OUR CAMP.
DAMN RED CROSS INSPECTORS! COMING TO FIND OUT WHAT HAS HAPPENED TO THE JEWS. AND THE ALLIES GETTING CLOSER. I WANT THIS PLACE BEAUTIFIED. AT ONCE!
WE MAKE A JEWISH PARADISE! THE FUHRER GIVES THE JEWS A TOWN!
FILL THE SHOPS! MEAT. BREAD. VEGETABLES. CLOTHES.
BREAD
GET RID OF THE THIRD TIER. IT MUST LOOK LIKE THESE 'HOMES' ARE COMFORTABLE, SPACIOUS.
AND - WE SEND A FEW MORE THOUSAND OF THEM EAST. WE DON'T WANT TO BE ACCUSED OF OVER-CROWDING!

THIS IS RADIO CUCKOOLAND FOR OUR TOWN, THE WORLD CLASS SPA. HERE ARE THE LATEST RUMOURS.
ANNOUNCEMENT. PAPA IS BEAUTIFYING OUR TOWN!.
1000 RED ROSES ROUND THE FOUNTAIN.
WHIPPED???
COFFEE WITH WHIPPED CREAM
MUSIC PAVILION
OFF-KEY!
WHITEWASHING OF WALLS. WHY?
THE FOREIGN PRESS MUST KNOW HOW GOOD PAPA IS TO US.
THANKS, PAPA!!!!
JUDE
JU

'S SCHOOL
TO THE PARK
THE CINEMA
POST OFFI
HE BANK
COFF
SAND PIT
TO CRECHE
Y GO ROUND
SAN
TO CRE
CRECHE. BUT THERE ARE NO BABIES LEFT!
WE'VE BECOME AN EXHIBIT! A STAGE-SET.

'SUDDENLY THERE RISES IN ME THE MOST TERRIBLE ANGER. IT IS LIKE A HUGE WAVE RISING FROM MY CENTRE, BURSTING, COMING OUT OF MY MOUTH LIKE SLAVER. HOW DARE THIS BLOWN-UP DEVIL DECIDE IF WE LIVE OR DIE. WE MUST DO SOMETHING!'

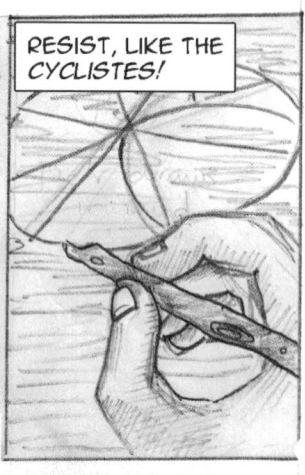

PLAY, LIKE THE GHETTO SWINGERS!

RESIST, LIKE THE CYCLISTES!

REMEMBER PIETR'S FATHER'S DEATH!

MY FATHER, SO POWERFUL, ONCE.

THEY ARE TRYING TO DESTROY EVIDENCE OF OUR EXISTENCE. THROWING INTO THE RIVER THE ASHES OF THOUSANDS.

LET'S DO SOMETHING.
MAKE SOMETHING.
TAKE BACK CONTROL.
MAKE SOMETHING THAT IS TRUE ABOUT US.
THEY'LL FIND OUT.
MY FATHER, I KEEP SEEING HIS FACE.
EVERYDAY HIS IMAGE GETS FAINTER. BUT HE MADE THINGS THAT I REMEMBER.
PUPPETS. WE MADE PLAYS WITH THEM TOGETHER AT HOME.

WHERE ARE THEY, THE PUPPETS?
IN DAD'S SUITCASE.
LET'S STEAL THEM!
YES - WE TOO CAN BE 'BAD'.
THE SUITCASE'S IN THE STORE OF CONFISCATED GOODS.
LET'S FIND THEM.
IT'S FORBIDDEN TO GO INTO THE STOREROOM.
A SECRET THEN. SWEAR!

DON'T YOU KNOW IT'S CURFEW? YOU WANT THE NEXT TRAIN EAST?
CIGGIES! AH! WHERE FROM?
THIS BLOKE. IF YOU LET HIM STROKE YOU.
GET ON WITH IT THEN. I'M SAYING NOTHING.
HURRY!
FORM A WALL. I'LL PICK THE LOCK.
CREEEEEEEEEKK

IS THAT A DEAD WOMAN? SKELETONS!
IS THAT A NAZI SPY OVER THERE? MUST BE A SHADOW.
THAT SHADOW'S A DRAGON!
A SUITCASE FULL OF TREASURE? OR IS IT DUST?

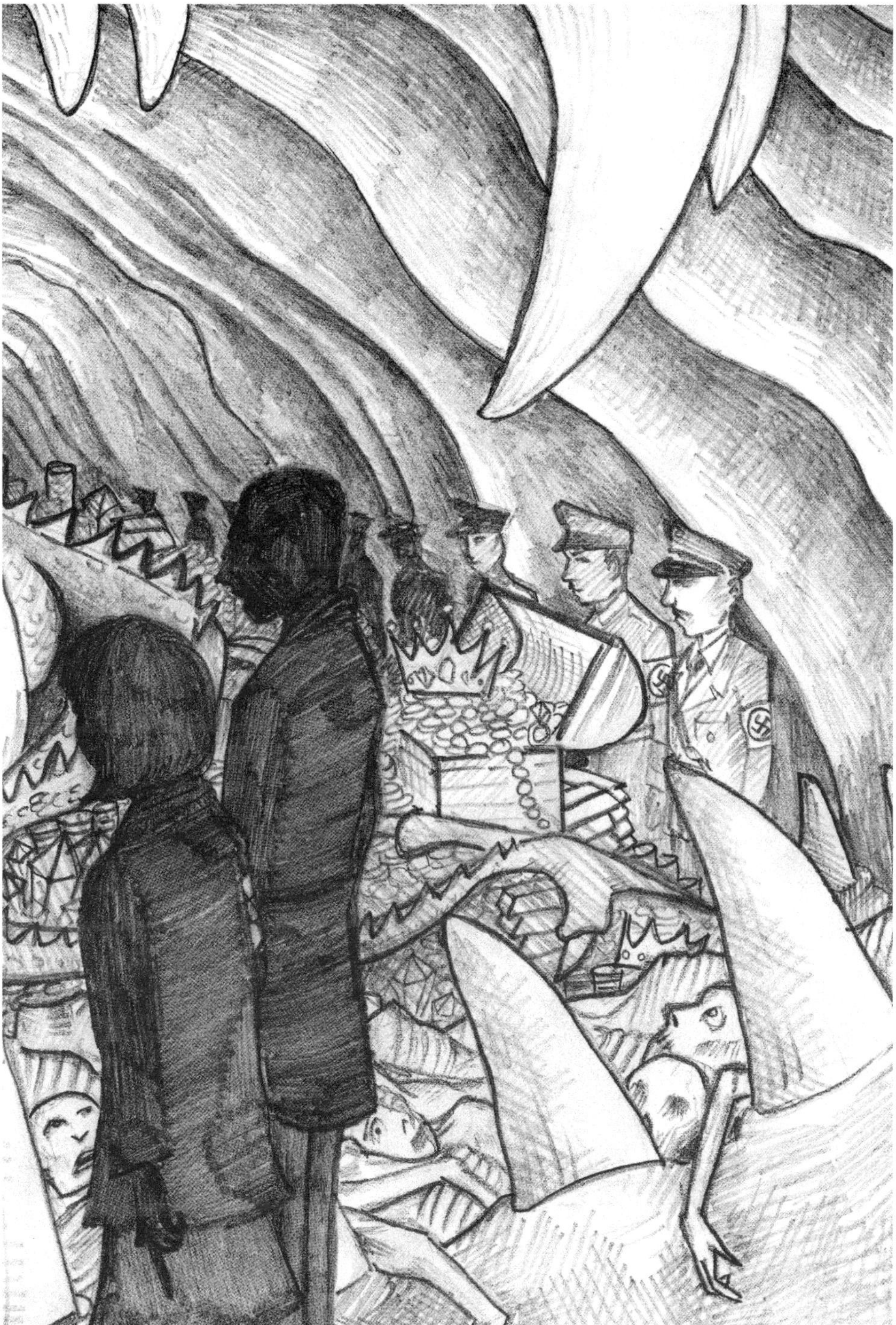

ALL THESE THINGS ARE LEFT BY THE DEAD.
I HATE THIS.
PHEW! IT STINKS.
LOOK FOR FOOD.
CLOTHES.
THEY'RE BEAUTIFUL.
AREN'T THEY FUNNY!
GOT THEM!
LET'S GO!

THE ATTIC! WE CAN HIDE HERE.
LOOK. A PIANO. IT'S LEGS ARE CUT OFF!
MAKE ANYTHING WE WANT.
IT STILL WORKS!
LET'S MAKE A PLAY
ABOUT BEING SAFE. ORDINARY.
NO! ABOUT OVERCOMING!
I'M MAKING MY OWN PUPPET TOO.
AREN'T THEY... SACRED. PART OF A CEREMONY.
THEY BELONG TO ANOTHER WORLD.
LET'S MAKE DREAMS.
A MAGIC MIRROR. A THIRD SPACE.
WHAT DOES IT WANT?
IT MAKES YOU FEEL SO POWERFUL.
HEY, YOU'VE MADE YOUR VOICE GO FUNNY.
HOW DO YOU MOVE IT?
'SO BEGAN ANOTHER WEIRD EXPERIENCE IN THIS LOST ISLAND. HOW TO MAKE ANOTHER SPEAK FOR ME.'

LET'S MAKE SHADOWS.
WE'RE IMPRISONED IN THIS CASTLE...
NO, A CAVE.
HA! I'M THE CLOCKWORK UBU, KING OF THE CASTLE.
BUT WE'RE GOING TO ESCAPE?
NO. KILL! KILL! POP OUT THEIR EYES. SLIT THEIR TONGUES.
STOP THAT! HAVE YOU GONE CRAZY?
SORRY. I LOST CONTROL.
HOW ARE WE GOING TO ESCAPE?

FLY, FLY OUT OF THE CAVE. OVER THE TERRIBLE WALLS.
I'M THE BIRD-ANGEL!
I D RATHER MELT INTO THE SPACE, THE SILENCE.
NO, FLY WITH ME, HIGH. WE'LL SWEEP OVER FOREST AND FIELDS.
WHAT CAN YOU SEE UP THERE?
THIS WAY HOME
ROADS. LORRIES, CARS. PEOPLE. A CROSS ROAD.
I'LL SEE GRANDMA'S DEAR FACE. OH THAT SMELL OF BAKING APPLE PIE!
GOULASH!
DUMPLINGS IN CHICKEN SOUP.
IN THE ORPHANAGE IT WAS MEAT ON SUNDAYS.

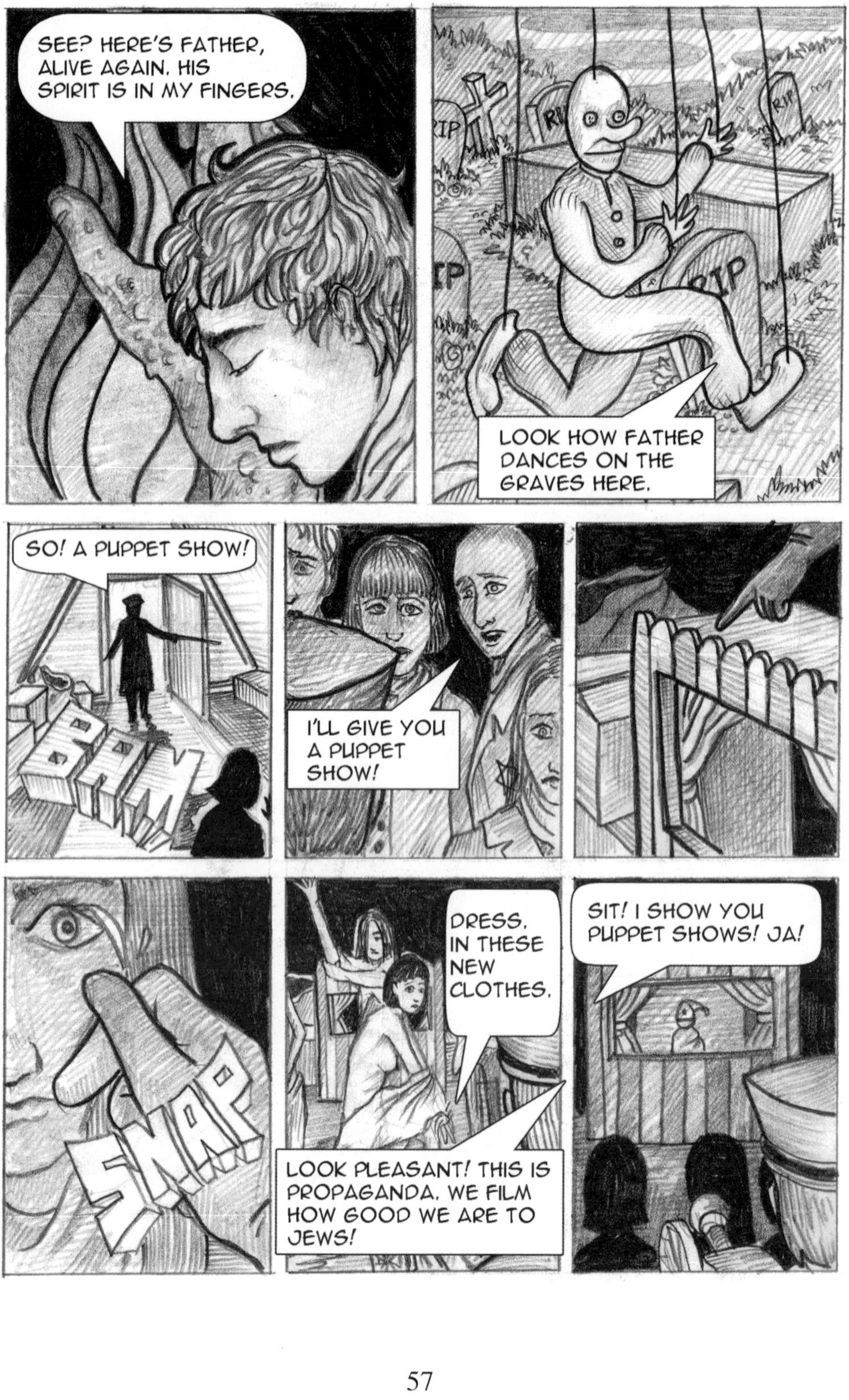
SEE? HERE'S FATHER, ALIVE AGAIN. HIS SPIRIT IS IN MY FINGERS.
LOOK HOW FATHER DANCES ON THE GRAVES HERE.
SO! A PUPPET SHOW!
I'LL GIVE YOU A PUPPET SHOW!
SNAP
DRESS. IN THESE NEW CLOTHES.
LOOK PLEASANT! THIS IS PROPAGANDA. WE FILM HOW GOOD WE ARE TO JEWS!
SIT! I SHOW YOU PUPPET SHOWS! JA!

SMILE, LONG NOSE. DAMN YOU!
DIE FUHRER SCHENKT DEN JUDEN EINE STADT. THE FUHRER GIVES THE JEWS A TOWN.
YOU! DIG! PLANT!
AND LOOK HAPPY!
NOW SEND THEM EAST!
GO WORK FOR THE REICH.

WRAP UP OUR PUPPETS.
HIDE THEM!
THEY WILL COME TO LIFE AGAIN.
MOVE! SCHNELL!
I CAN'T LET YOU GO ALONE, BOYS.. I'M YOUR CARER. I'M COMING WITH YOU.
THE RAILWAY STATION, THERESIENSTADT.
CAN YOU SEE THEM?

THEY'RE GOING.

YOU WANT TO COME TOO?

'THEN THE GERMANS STARTED PULLING OUT. THE TRANSPORTS FROM THERESIENSTADT STOPPED. THERE WAS PLENTY OF ROOM FOR EVERYONE NOW. IT WAS A DESOLATE PLACE. ALL WE WANTED WAS TO LIE DOWN, BUT WE WERE DESPERATE TO KEEP ALIVE. WE LUGGED TREE TRUNKS, SHOVELLED COAL FROM THE WAGONS.. WE COOKED POTATOES FROM SACKS WE FOUND. ALL GERMANS HAD GONE - COOKS, WARDERS. WE FELT SULLEN, ANGRY. WHY THEM AND NOT US? THEN ONE DAY IN MAY... IT WAS 1945...'

GREETINGS!
THE RUSSIANS ARE HERE!
THE WAR IS OVER!
YOU MUST EAT SOMETHING.
YOU ARE FREE PERSONS. YOU MAY GO HOME.
SAY THERE'S NO ONE LEFT AT HOME?
HOME? WHERE'S THAT?
YOU CAN REGISTER TO GO TO PALESTINE.
WOULD YOU LIKE TO GO TO ENGLAND? WE WILL TAKE YOU TO PRAGUE AIRPORT. A PLANE WILL TAKE YOU OUT. WE WILL FIND YOU A HOME.
GIVE THEM ONLY SWEATENED TEA.

'THEN SUDDENLY, GONDA WAS GONE. SHE DECIDED TO WALK OUT OF THE CAMP, TO WALK HOME. SHE DISAPPEARED, WITHOUT SAYING A WORD TO ME. I KNEW SHE SIMPLY WANTED TO GO HOME. I DIDN'T BLAME HER. BUT LIFE WITH OUT HER WAS MORE BLEAK THAN LIFE WITHOUT ARIE.DID SHE MAKE IT HOME? I WILLED THIS WITH ALL MY STRENGTH.'
HOP IN. WHERE ARE YOU GOING?
TO MY UNCLE'S HOUSE IN PRAGUE.
I DON'T KNOW IF MY PARENTS ARE ALIVE.
OH! MRS KOVA!

RESIST! REFORM THE FUTURE!!!
'I TOO, WANTED TO GET BACK HOME. MY CLEVER COMPUTER HAD GOT ME HERE SO I COULD UNDERSTAND WHAT LIFE COULD BE LIKE OUTSIDE OUR ELECTRONIC GATES. OF EXURBIA, AMERCITY. I HAD BEEN GIVEN THE CHANCE TO GROW UP, EVEN THOUGH AT GREAT COST. BUT DESPITE LOSING ARIE, I HAD DISCOVERED THE NATURE OF LOVE, OF DEATH AND HOW TO MAKE SOMETHING OUT OF NOTHING. I FINALLY REALISED I HAD LEARNED THAT ONLY FREEDOM AND KINDNESS MATTERED. I SEEMED TO LIVE IN A DIFFERENT WORLD FROM MY PARENTS NOW. IT WAS UP TO ME TO FIND A WAY OF JOINING THEM UP... A NEW WAY.

CHERRIES IN THE ICEBOX
CONTEMPORARY HEBREW SHORT STORIES

ed *Marion Baraitser* and *Haya Hoffman*
Introduction by Haya Hoffman
With The European Jewish Publication Society

Papaerback   ISBN: 0 9529426 5 8   £11.50

A unique collection of twelve of the best, daring, young multicultural voices, writing in Hebrew today, these stories encapsulate the diverse mosaic of a society that is uncomfortable with itself, as it comes to terms with violence and dislocation, with wry wit and hope that counters despair.

'**Excellent and stimulating anthology**' — *Jewish Chronicle*

'The easiest way to find out who will be the next Amos Oz' — *Jewish Renaissance*

LOKI INTERNATIONAL PLAY SERIES

- *ECHOES OF ISRAEL: **Contemporary Drama***
  ed. *Marion Baraitser*
  Paperback   ISBN: 0 9529426 3 1   £9.99

From the Royal National Theatre.

'Bold dramas...revealing the rifts and taboos in Israeli society at this crucial time in the nation's history.' *New Statesman*

A FAMILY STORY by Edna Mazya
Winner of the Israeli Theatre Award 1997/8 (see over page)

MURDER by **Hanoch Levin**
Play of the year and Playwright of the Year, 1997
SHEINDALE by **Rami Danon** and **Amnon Levy**
'A vital subject .. an intriguing merciless play' Al Ha'Mish Mar
MR MANI, a monodrama by **A.B. Yehoshua**. *'A fascinating insight into the British presence in Palestine by the Israel Prize winner.'* Ha'aretz

- **BOTTLED NOTES FROM UNDERGROUND: CONTEMPORARY PLAYS BY JEWISH WRITERS**
  ed **Linden S, Baraitser M.**
  Paperback   ISBN: 0 9529426 2 3   £9.99

From Sobol to Schneider—a barn-breaking collection of five popular award-winning new plays of excellence from London, New York and Israel. Features Israel's greatest living playwright
JOSHUA SOBOL's *The Palestinian Girl*
with **Carole Braverman, Marion Baraitser, Sonja Linden,** and **David Schneider.**

- **THE DEFIANT MUSE: HEBREW FEMINIST POEMS FROM ANTIQUITY TO THE PRESENT: A BILINGUAL ANTHOLOGY**

Ed *Shirley Kaufman, Galit Hasan-Rokem,* and *Tamar Hess*
Paperback   ISBN: 0 9529426 4 X   £12.99

Poetry Book Society Recommended Translation, 2000

Unprecedented in its scope, many of these poems are unknown to an English speaking audience. A unique volume of 100 poems by 50 writers from antiquity to the present, which transforms the perception of Jewish women's poetry in Hebrew.

- Unique bilingual anthology transforming the conception of Jewish women's poetry.
- New material, new translations.
- Introduction placing the poems in historical, cultural, and literary perspectives, and full bibliographic and biographical notes.
- Arts Council of England and European Jewish Publication Society support. Published in association with The Feminist Press at CUNY

Shirley Kaufman: prize-winning American Israeli poet and translator who has published seven volumes of poems, as well as translations from Hebrew and Dutch.
Galit Hasan-Rokem: professor of folklore at the Hebrew University of Jerusalem, translator, scholar, and poet: **Tamar Hess**: teacher at the Hebrew University.

All books available from good book shops or from amazon.co.uk, or LokiBook s,38ChalcotCrescent,LondonNW1 8YD:all@lokibooks.vianw.co.uk http://www. lokibooks.u-net.com. Trade: Central Books.99 Wallis Rd, London E9 5LN: tel: +44 (0)845 4589911 : fax:+44 (0)845 4589912: orders@centralbooks.com